D1094949

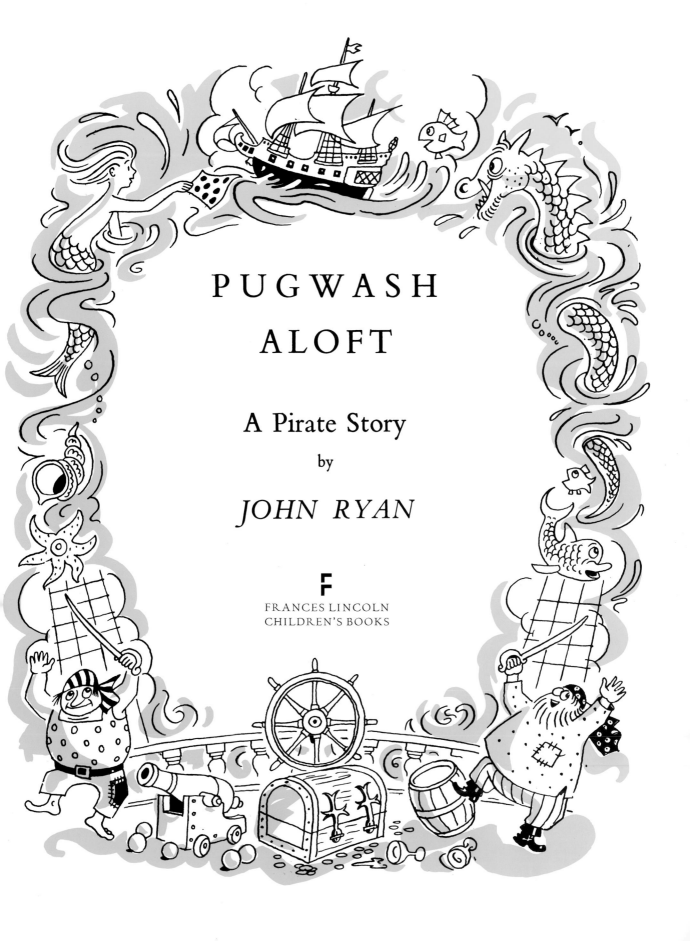

PUGWASH
ALOFT

A Pirate Story

by

JOHN RYAN

F

FRANCES LINCOLN
CHILDREN'S BOOKS

It was a warm, sunny evening, and Captain Pugwash had decided to take a day off from sailing. He had found a smooth part of the sea, sheltered from the waves by a large treasure island and there his ship, *The Black Pig,* lay, rocking gently at anchor. It was just the weather for sleeping or playing or fishing

but for once the pirates weren't doing any of these things, for the Captain had got them all together on the poop deck for a singing practice. And it was *not* going very well. 'No, no, no!' he cried. 'You'll never make good pirates unless you can sing a sea shanty properly! Tom! Give 'em the tune again!'

So little Tom, the cabin boy, played the tune on his concertina and the pirates patted their chests, cleared their throats and began to sing :—

'And away boys away!

Away to Rio.

So fare you well

My pretty young girl

For we're off to the Rio Grande!'

Now the Captain wasn't very happy about the singing, but he would have been far less happy had he known what was going on down below.

Cut-throat Jake, the most terrible pirate afloat, had been hiding in his ship on the other side of the island, and now, with a crew of dreadful desperadoes, he was rowing very stealthily right up to *The Black Pig*. And Cut-throat Jake was Captain Pugwash's worst enemy.

'Heh, heh, heh!' muttered Jake in a throaty whisper. 'Just listen to 'em . . . *singing*. I'll give that old scally-wag something to sing about! Scramble up the sides, boys! They're going to get the shock o' their lives in a minute! Heh, heh!'

So Jake's pirates climbed very quietly out of their long-boat . . .

and a moment after, they
slipped silently on to the
deck of *The Black Pig*.
'Now we'll have some sport, me hearties,' whispered Jake.
'Didn't know I could sing, did you?' And neither Pugwash
nor his crew noticed anything odd happening as Jake

and his men
sneaked silently
behind them ...
and joined in
the singing.

'That's better,' cried Captain Pugwash, conducting like anything. 'Now you sound like twice as many pirates.'

Then
suddenly
he
stopped . . .

and the music stopped. And the Captain looked . . . and saw that there *were* twice as many pirates.

'Jump on 'em!'
roared Cut-
throat Jake. 'We've got
'em where we want 'em
now boys!' and a moment later the deck of *The Black
Pig* was covered with rival pirates kicking and biting,
scratching and fighting.

Now Captain Pugwash's men weren't much good at this kind of thing, and very soon Jake's men had them all trussed up and quite helpless. And the Captain himself had such a time at the hands of Cut-throat Jake that it wasn't long before he turned and ran away as fast as he could go.

And as there aren't many places you can escape to on a ship, he made for the nearest mast and started to climb up . . . up and away from the enemy pirates.

High above the deck he felt a little safer, but down at the bottom of the mast, Cut-throat Jake shook his great fist and shouted; 'You won't escape me that way! I'll climb up too . . . and throw you into the sea with me own hands I will. Hah-harrh!'

Now it happened that nobody had taken any notice of Tom because he was only a cabin boy. But Tom had been watching everything, and had thought of a clever plan to save Pugwash.

'Please, Captain Jake,' he called. 'I've got a much better idea, and it'll save you a lot of trouble. Why not *saw* the mast down?' And he held up the biggest saw he could find on the ship.

'Well . . . Blow me down!'
said Jake. 'It's that cabin boy
of his. That's a very good idea
of yours; I'll make a pirate of
you yet, me lad.'
'Right-ho, Captain,' said Tom.
'Here you are. I'll help you.'

So after they had put all Pugwash's pirates down below, Cut-throat Jake's men gathered round eagerly to watch as Jake and little Tom began to saw.

High
at the top
of his mast
Captain Pugwash
heard the noise
and thought
that his last hour
had really
arrived.

'It's
coming,'
roared Jake.
'It's
coming . . .
Down she comes!'

And with a terrible,
rending, tearing
noise . . .

down came
the mast.

But there were two things that Cut-throat Jake in his excitement hadn't noticed. The first was, that when the mast came down, it would snare him and all his pirates in a fearful tangle of ropes and spars.

And the second thing Jake hadn't noticed was that Tom, who had been very careful to get out of the way, had tricked him into sawing down the wrong mast. So, while Jake and all his men were struggling helplessly under the fallen mast . . .

Captain Pugwash was still clinging on, quite safe,
to the top of the next one.

'It's all right, Cap'n, you can come down now!' called Tom, and down came Pugwash even faster than he went up. And a moment later

he was standing in triumph over Cut-throat Jake.

And then they untied all Captain Pugwash's pirates and tied up Jake and all his, and Tom rolled them over the side of *The Black Pig* so that they fell 'Plop!' back into their own long-boat.

And there they left them,
struggling and kicking and
quite unable to do anything.
But *The Black Pig* sailed away
with Captain Pugwash and his
men feeling so pleased with
themselves

That they sang for all they were worth and danced for joy.

And Tom, the cabin boy, just smiled to himself as he played on his concertina . . . and said nothing.

First published in 1958 by The Bodley Head Ltd
This edition published in Great Britain in 2007 and in the USA in 2008
by Frances Lincoln Children's Books, 4 Torriano Mews,
Torriano Avenue, London NW5 2RZ
www.franceslincoln.com

ISBN 978-1-84507-822-5

Printed in China

1 3 5 7 9 8 6 4 2